A
B

Pirate Nap

A Book of COLORS

by DANNA SMITH

Illustrated by VALERIA PETRONE

Clarion Books • Houghton Mifflin Harcourt • Boston New York 2011

CLARION BOOKS
215 Park Avenue South
New York, New York 10003

Clarion Books is an imprint of Houghton Mifflin Harcourt Publishing Company.

www.hmhbooks.com

The text of this book is set in Shannon.
The illustrations were executed in digital gouache.

Library of Congress Cataloging-in-Publication Data

Smith, Danna.
Pirate nap : a book of colors / by Danna Smith ; illustrated by Valeria Petrone.
p. cm.
Summary: Two brothers use their imaginations to turn their surroundings—from a white bandanna and yellow coins to a red blanket and even their baby sister—into a colorful pirate adventure before naptime.
ISBN 978-0-547-57531-5
[1. Stories in rhyme. 2. Color—Fiction. 3. Pirates—Fiction. 4. Imagination—Fiction. 5. Brothers—Fiction. 6. Play—Fiction.] I. Petrone, Valeria, ill. II. Title.
PZ8.3.S6492Pi 2011
[E]—dc22
2010043253

Manufactured in China
LEO 10 9 8 7 6 5 4 3 2 1
4500294823

For Dave, my husband and best friend —D.S.

To my brother, Fabio, and our old-time games and adventures —V.P.

Afternoon on Spyglass Street.
Pirates fighting in bare feet.

WHITE bandanna. One good eye.
Pirates plunder. Pirates spy.

Raid a hideout. Do a jig.

Feast on grub. Guzzle. Swig.

YELLOW treasures buried deep.
Lucky pirates. Loot to keep!

“Time for a nap, rowdy crew.
Mighty pirates need sleep, too.”

Captain sneers. "'Tis a trap!
Pirates never, ever nap!"

No surrender! Coming through.
Lots of pirate things to do.

Find the ship in the bay.
Look for treasures on the way.

Creeping. Quiet. Sword in hand.
Search the rugged open land.

Avast! A mountain up ahead.
Dig up treasure. Fluffy. **RED!**

Spider webs and shadows grow.
Follow the map where breezes blow.

Mark the spot. We must be brave!
Find GREEN treasure in a cave.

Another clue. Blow me down!
A treasure chest! Wooden. **BROWN.**

Pirate's luck. The treasure's big.
Yo ho ho! The pirates dig.

Singing sailors. Hidden cove.
Thar it be—a treasure trove!

Sparkling jewels. ORANGE beads.
All the things a pirate needs!

Hear a scream. What could it be?
A **PURPLE** monster from the sea!

It grabs the loot. A dirty trick!
Catch the monster! Hurry! Quick!

See the ship. Home at last.

Raise the **BLACK** flag on the mast.

Tumble in. Climb aboard.
Stash the treasures. Stow the sword.

Lift the anchor. Pull the hitch.
Happy pirates. Sleepy. Rich!

Calm BLUE water. Briny deep.
Pirates, monster, sail to sleep.